SPACE SCOUT ™

SCOUTING THE UNIVERSE FOR A NEW EARTH

The Jelly People
published in 2010 by
Hardie Grant Egmont
85 High Street
Prahran, Victoria 3181, Australia
www.hardiegrantegmont.com.au

Hardie Grant Egmont uses
Greenhouse Friendly™
ENVI Carbon Neutral Paper

ENVI Carbon Neutral Paper is an Australian Government
certified Greenhouse Friendly™ Product.

The text for this book has been printed on ENVI Carbon Neutral Paper.

A CiP record for this title is available from the National Library of Australia

Text copyright © 2010 H. Badger
Series, illustration and design copyright © 2010 Hardie Grant Egmont

Cover illustration by D. Mackie
Illustrated by C. Bennett
Design by S. Swingler
Typeset by Ektavo
Printed in Australia by McPherson's Printing Group

1 3 5 7 9 10 8 6 4 2

THE JELLY PEOPLE

BY **H. BADGER**

ILLUSTRATED BY **C. BENNETT**

hardie grant EGMONT

CHAPTER 1

Kip Kirby hated not being good at things. And he especially hated being the very worst in the class!

It was Saturday morning and Kip was at Dino-Training class. His pet minisaur Duke just *wouldn't* roll over.

Minisaurs were knee-high brontosauruses. They were bred as family pets

from fossil DNA. A giant company called WorldCorp had invented them a while ago, back in the year 2328.

Kip sometimes wondered what it was like in the olden days. Kip had read that back then, kids had dogs and cats as pets.

Bet a dog wouldn't chew two pairs of expensive spaceboots in one week, Kip thought.

'Roll over, Duke!' he said. 'Come on!'

But instead, Duke jumped into Kip's arms. He licked Kip's face with his slobbery dinosaur tongue.

'I know your brain's smaller than a freeze-dried pea,' Kip laughed. 'But this is ridiculous!'

It was hard to stay mad at Duke, even

if everyone in the AirPark was staring at them.

The AirPark was a huge area covered in fake grass. It was high up in the sky, on top of a sky scraper.

AirParks had replaced ground-level parks ages ago. With a population of over a trillion people, there just wasn't room on Earth anymore.

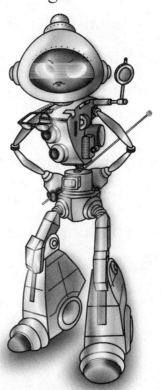

Over the excited roaring of the class of minisaurs, Kip heard the Teacherbot call out.

'Time to practise using your sonic leashes,' the Teacherbot chirped.

The Teacherbot was a basic worker robot with special patience software installed. This one was as tall as Kip, and was made of soft, waterproof plastic to protect against minisaur bites and slobber.

Kip grabbed his sonic leash from his pocket. He clipped the flashing collar around Duke's neck. Then he flicked on the remote-control unit.

Unlike old-fashioned leashes, there was nothing joining Duke's collar to Kip's hand.

If Kip selected Turn Right on his remote control, the collar would make a high-

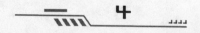

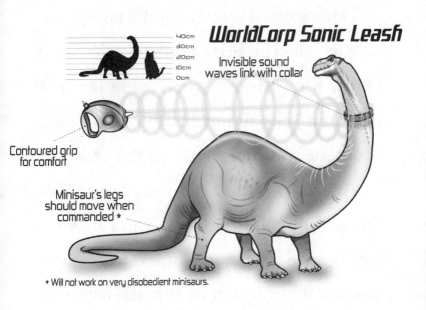

WorldCorp Sonic Leash

40cm
30cm
20cm
10cm
0cm

Invisible sound
waves link with collar

Contoured grip
for comfort

Minisaur's legs
should move when
commanded *

* Will not work on very disobedient minisaurs.

frequency sound only Duke could hear. Then Duke would turn right. At least, that's what was *supposed* to happen…

'Tell your minisaur to walk straight ahead!' called the Teacherbot.

Kip selected Walk Straight Ahead.

Duke started scratching the fake grass.

Kip rolled his eyes. As much as he loved Duke, Kip just didn't have time for this. Between school and his job as a Space Scout, he was super-busy all the time.

At 12, Kip was the youngest ever Space Scout. Tests showed Kip's bravery, intelligence and physical fitness were better than 99.9999% of those tested. That's why he'd been hired by WorldCorp to explore the galaxies for a second Earth to live on.

Kip wanted to discover Earth 2 more than anything. And so did the 49 other Space Scouts. Discovering Earth 2 would win a Space Scout the ultimate prize – the Shield of Honour.

Kip often imagined how brilliant winning would feel. As well as the glory, Kip loved the sound of the other prizes that came with the Shield – like a mansion on Earth 2! And WorldCorp had just added another awesome prize – an extra day off school or work every week.

The Teacherbot interrupted Kip's daydream. 'Tell your minisaur to walk faster!'

Kip turned up the speed dial on his sonic leash's remote control. Of course, Duke chose that exact moment to fall asleep.

But Kip hardly noticed. His SpaceCuff was buzzing!

A SpaceCuff was a thick silver band worn

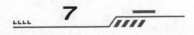

on the wrist. It had a built-in screen. Space Scouts used SpaceCuffs to communicate with their starships and WorldCorp.

Kip pressed the Open Message button on his SpaceCuff.

It was a mission brief. Excitement shot up Kip's spine. He was off to space again!

SPACE SCOUT KIP KIRBY MISSION BRIEF

Message from: WorldCorp Mission Control

WorldCorp has received coded messages about an unexplored planet called Aquaron. It seems Aquaron is trading something very valuable with other planets.

Therefore, WorldCorp believes Aquaron has natural resources that may be useful to humans.

The source of the messages is unknown.

Your mission:

Explore Aquaron, find out what is being traded and collect samples. Work out whether humans could live on Aquaron.

Go to the Intergalactic Hoverport and prepare for immediate departure.

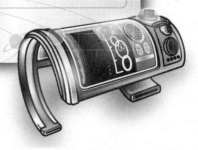

CHAPTER 2

WorldCorp wanted Kip to leave immediately. Kip guessed a wormhole to Aquaron must have opened unexpectedly. Wormholes were shortcuts from one galaxy to another. Space Scouts could travel millions of light years in seconds. But wormholes never stayed open for long.

'I've got to leave early,' Kip apologised

to the Teacherbot. A sad-face emoticon popped up on the Teacherbot's screen.

Once Kip and Duke got back down to ground level, Kip scratched Duke's scaly head. 'Go home, boy,' he said.

Duke trotted off towards Kip's apartment. Kip couldn't believe it.

Maybe Dino-Training is working after all! he thought, racing to the nearest Rocket Bus stop. A Rocket Bus heading for the Hoverport would be along any second.

All space flights left from the Intergalactic Hoverport. It hovered inside Earth's atmosphere, about 10 kilometres above the ground.

Rummaging in his backpack, Kip

grabbed his spacesuit, boots and helmet. Luckily, he had them with him. He was supposed to drop them at WorldCorp's cleaning department after Dino-Training.

Kip's spacesuit was green, as were his matching boots. Made of soft, meteor-proof fabric, the suit was designed to fit Kip perfectly. He got a new one every couple of missions. Kip's helmet had sparkling red flames on the side.

Making sure no-one was looking, Kip stepped into his spacesuit. As a Space Scout, Kip prided himself on always being in control. Getting changed at a bus stop didn't *quite* fit that image.

Kip had just finished changing when a

Space Scout #50: Kip Kirby

bus plummeted through the air towards him.

Rocket Buses looked like old-fashioned buses, except they were standing on their end. The driver stopped smoothly, hovering half a metre above the stop. Kip climbed a ladder to get inside.

Instead of seats, the Rocket Bus had harnesses on the walls. Kip locked his waist, neck and ankle straps into position.

The bus shot up into the air so fast that Kip's whole body was thrown against the wall.

Awesome g-force! Kip thought. No matter how often he blasted into the atmosphere on a Rocket Bus, he never got sick of it.

Kip was enjoying himself so much that he didn't notice an extra passenger had sneaked on board. Until a scaly green shape shot past his nose...

Kip blinked. *Was that a flying minisaur?*

Then Kip realised. Instead of going home, Duke had followed him onto the bus.

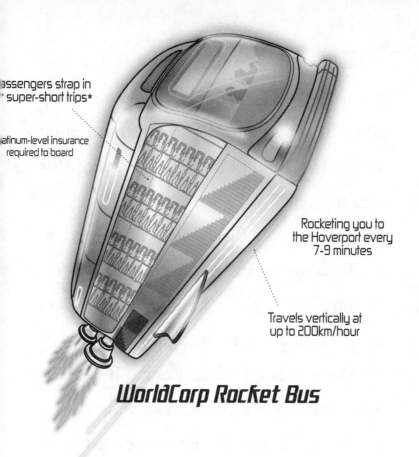

assengers strap in
super-short trips*

atinum-level insurance
required to board

Rocketing you to
the Hoverport every
7-9 minutes

Travels vertically at
up to 200km/hour

WorldCorp Rocket Bus

Using every one of his carefully trained

Space Scout muscles, Kip ripped his hands

from the walls. He wriggled his arms free

of the harness. Then Kip lunged for Duke

as he flew past again.

I'll have to take him on the mission, Kip thought as he slipped his safety strap around Duke. He couldn't miss the wormhole for one minisaur!

The Rocket Bus was so fast that Kip soon arrived at the Hoverport.

The Hoverport looked like a giant carpark floating in space. But instead of anything as low-tech as Rocket Buses, the Hoverport was filled with starships.

The smaller starships travelled to nearby planets like Venus. The bigger ones, like Kip's starship MoNa 4000, travelled far beyond the Milky Way.

MoNa was a black, multi-level starship

with curved thrusters and glowing lights underneath. When he saw her, Kip spoke into his SpaceCuff.

'Kip Kirby to MoNa 4000. Approaching Hoverport.'

'At last,' grumbled MoNa.

Kip grinned. As usual, MoNa was in a terrible mood.

He pulled the cord and the Rocket Bus stopped right beside MoNa's landing bay. It was freezing cold and the air was thin up here, but Kip would be fine with his spacesuit on.

But what about Duke?

'Sorry, boy,' he said, stuffing Duke into his backpack. It sealed perfectly. It would

keep Duke warm enough to survive the short skywalk.

Kip left the Rocket Bus and quickly jumped into MoNa's landing bay.

'Your backpack!' said a friendly, deep voice. 'I think it's alive.'

Finbar, Kip's second-in-command (or 2iC for short), had come to the landing bay to meet him.

Finbar was two metres tall, and was a cross between a human and an arctic wolf. Normally, he was the only animal on Space Scout missions.

Wonder if he'll mind having a naughty minisaur along for the ride, Kip grinned to himself.

CHAPTER 3

Duke jumped out of Kip's backpack. Finbar bent down and tickled him under the chin.

What a softie! Kip thought.

Finbar was an Animaul, bred to protect Earth from alien invaders. But Finbar was so gentle that he'd failed Animaul training. WorldCorp reassigned him to be Kip's

2iC. Finbar was calm and wise, not daring like Kip. His sharp wolf senses and loyalty made up for it, though.

'That creature is distracting you both,' came MoNa's voice. She saw and heard everything Kip and Finbar did.

'The wormhole to Aquaron is open,' MoNa continued. 'In case you haven't noticed, I used my auto-pilot to leave the Hoverport. But you're needed at the controls right away.'

Frowning, Kip left the landing bay. Space Scouting would be heaps more fun without a bossy starship!

Kip and Finbar strode along MoNa's glowing blue corridors. With Duke at their feet, they headed for the bridge, MoNa's control centre.

At the round door to the bridge, a security laser scanned Kip's eyeball. Only then were Kip and Finbar allowed inside.

The bridge had sloping walls and a big window that was now looking over Earth. Kip and Finbar sat down in the padded chairs in the middle.

Kip touched the air above his head. A blue holographic cylinder beamed down from above. Kip and Finbar were surrounded by it. MoNa's controls were projected onto the cylinder.

Expertly, Kip switched MoNa from auto-pilot mode. He took the controls

himself. Flying a starship was tough, but Kip had studied intensively. In Space Scout training, Flying was his favourite subject.

Soon, a strange, swirling red cloud loomed into view. The wormhole!

They powered forward into the cloud. Colours exploded all around. Kip's head ached and his skin prickled. Finbar turned green with space-sickness.

But in 3.2 seconds, the trip through the wormhole was over. MoNa popped out into Aquaron's galaxy.

Wobbly legged, Finbar walked to the windows. A large, bright red planet filled one entire window. Aquaron!

Kip felt the nervous thrill he always got

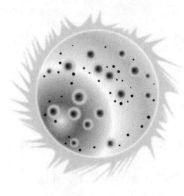 when he was about to land on a brand-new planet.

Space Scouts were trained to deal with the unknown. Tackling new challenges was one of the reasons Kip loved the job.

Kip took in every detail of Aquaron. As a Space Scout, it was important to notice as much as possible.

'Earth's got green patches of land,' Kip said. 'But this planet's completely red.'

'My long-range telescopes say Aquaron's covered with water,' MoNa said.

Finbar yelped. 'An ocean planet? Wolves hate swimming!'

'Go to the landing bay,' MoNa said, ignoring him. 'A WaterWalker is waiting.'

Kip had read about WaterWalkers in his Space Scout Vehicle Manual. They were clear, oxygen-filled capsules with motors.

Kip wouldn't be wearing his spacesuit on this mission. He took it off and slipped on a SeaStocking over his normal clothes – a thin, transparent suit that was better for swimming in than his spacesuit.

I didn't have to get changed at the bus-stop after all! he groaned to himself.

When they were ready, Kip and Finbar headed for the landing bay. Kip wondered how the WaterWalker would get down to Aquaron.

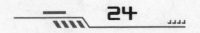

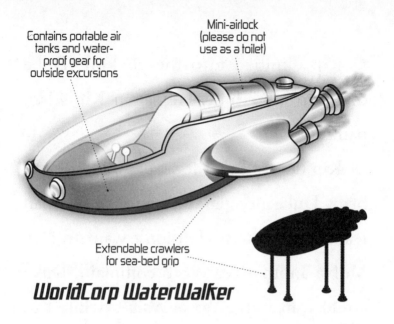

Contains portable air tanks and water-proof gear for outside excursions

Mini-airlock (please do not use as a toilet)

Extendable crawlers for sea-bed grip

WorldCorp WaterWalker

Normally, MoNa beamed Kip and Finbar to new planets using her Scrambler Beams. Scramblers took your particles, scrambled them, and then rearranged them on the surface of the destination planet.

'I'll shoot the WaterWalker into the Aquaron ocean,' MoNa explained when they reached the landing bay.

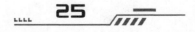

Kip climbed into the cockpit. Duke dived in after him. He sat in Kip's lap, panting.

Kip decided that it would be better to bring Duke along in the WaterWalker than leave him behind. He didn't want to give MoNa another reason to complain. Duke could wait in the WaterWalker while Kip scouted Aquaron.

Kip fitted his safety harness over himself as well as Duke. Finbar strapped in behind them. The WaterWalker's watertight doors sealed shut.

The floor beneath the WaterWalker began to vibrate. Duke's bony tail flicked side-to-side, smacking Kip in the face.

'Stop it, Du –' Kip started to say.
Then...

AAAAAAHHH!

The landing bay floor dropped away below them. The WaterWalker went hurtling at top speed through space!

The starry sky rushed past in a blur. The WaterWalker shot through Aquaron's atmosphere with a bump. Split-seconds later, they splashed into Aquaron's bright red sea.

Kip gasped. The sea was rough, but it wasn't like oceans on Earth. Instead, Aquaron's red water churned in a gigantic whirlpool. And Kip, Finbar and Duke had landed right in the middle!

 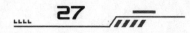

CHAPTER 4

The whirlpool spun them around and sucked them downwards.

Faster and faster they whirled around, until Kip wanted to throw up. Finbar actually did! Luckily Finbar used a stink-proof SpaceSick Bag that was stored in the WaterWalker.

As they spun around, Kip caught a

glimpse of his SpaceCuff. *Uh-oh, there's no reception underwater,* he realised.

There was no way to tell MoNa what was happening.

The entire world was red and murky. The whirlpool blew sand everywhere. In the gloom, Kip saw that the water teemed with thick, wriggling black slugs.

Giant leeches! he thought. Kip had been trained to deal with creepy creatures. But leeches were especially yucky. They sucked your blood until they were bloated with it.

At least, that's what leeches do on Earth, Kip thought. *Giant alien leeches might be even worse!*

Without warning, the whirlpool

suddenly stopped. The sandy water cleared.

The whirlpool had sucked the WaterWalker down to the sea floor. Directly in front lay a massive transparent dome. Inside the dome, glittering black towers soared upwards from the sand.

Something valuable is being traded on Aquaron, Kip remembered. *It could come from this underwater city.*

But could humans ever live under the sea? With a fresh air supply, maybe. It was definitely worth looking around. For the first time since landing on Aquaron, Kip fired up the WaterWalker's engine.

Finbar spotted what looked like the main entrance to the city. On either side,

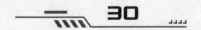

there were two massive propellers. The blades were still, but the sand around the towers had been blown away.

Those propellers must have been used recently, Kip thought.

Then Kip noticed something else. There was a pair of eels guarding the city entrance. Like the leeches, they were thousands of times bigger than any eel on Earth. They were bigger than Rocket Buses!

The eels had dagger-sharp teeth. Thick black liquid dripped from them, spreading inky clouds through the water.

Kip gazed at the transparent dome and the glittering city inside. It would be tough, but he was determined to sneak past the

ALIEN EELS

Size varies between planets – can be as big as a bus.

Found on most planets with water due to the eels' excellent adaptation skills.

Easily trained, they are useful guards.

FILE: EELS

monster eels and into the city.

'Look!' said Finbar suddenly.

The eels had spotted the WaterWalker! Strangely, it looked like they were using their tails to wave Kip and Finbar inside.

Space Scout training had taught Kip to trust his instincts. This time, though, his instincts had told him the eels weren't friendly. *Instincts can be wrong sometimes*, he thought.

Kip piloted the WaterWalker through the automatic doors in the side of the dome. Finbar rummaged for OxyGlobes and flippers in the WaterWalker's supply cupboard.

'You need to stay here, boy,' Kip said firmly to Duke.

Duke whined. His big brown eyes were seriously sad, but Kip knew it could be dangerous to take Duke with him. Kip patted his minisaur goodbye and opened up the hatch.

He and Finbar climbed out the back of

the Water Walker through the mini-airlock. Duke whined again as Kip shut the door firmly behind them. Finbar looked like he wanted to take Duke with him, too.

Once they were out in the water, walking along the seabed was difficult. The water SeaStockings had some weights inside to stop them from floating back up to the surface. But the weights also made every step feel heavy. It was easier for Kip and Finbar to half-walk, half-swim their way along.

Kip soon stopped noticing, though. The underwater city was spread out in front of them. Kip took in every dazzling detail. Thousands of towers rose up from the

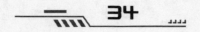

sand. The buildings weren't made of super-strength glass like Kip's apartment tower on Earth. Instead, they were covered in glossy black pearl. The towers were wide at the bottom and pointy at the top.

Between the towers were tall poles, poking up from the sand. Each pole had a small rotating dish on top. A blue light on each one blinked every few seconds.

But the city wasn't just high-tech. It looked like fun, too. In a single street, Kip spotted lots of things that humans would like – a fun park, cinemas, restaurants and a bowling alley. The sign out the front of the alley showed a jellyfish holding a bowling ball in each tentacle.

The aliens here are pretty advanced, Kip noted. *And they must like to have fun.*

Kip loved Space Scouting. How else would he get to visit cool places like this underwater city? But sometimes he wished he could hang out more when he travelled. Instead, it was all work from the moment he arrived.

Everywhere Kip looked, there were dull grey bushes with square leaves.

Not the nicest-looking plants, Kip noted. *So why are they growing everywhere?*

'Let's explore,' Finbar said.

Kip nodded. 'Keep your eyes peeled for something worth trading, and –'

'Not so fast, Earthling,' said a voice

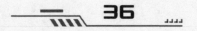

behind Kip.

Kip spun around. Behind him was what *looked* like a giant floating jellyfish!

'My name is Nurdor,' the alien said in perfect English.

Kip tried not to show his surprise. He'd never met an alien who could speak his language before.

'Welcome to the Kingdom of the Jelly People,' said Nurdor with a strange smile. 'But please, call us Jellies.'

CHAPTER 5

Nurdor's entire body was transparent. His head and tentacles looked like they were made of gooey jelly. Instead of legs, he had a billowing skirt like a jellyfish.

He glowed pale blue, and was much bigger than Kip. Unlike a jellyfish on Earth, he seemed to have a skeleton made of jelly inside.

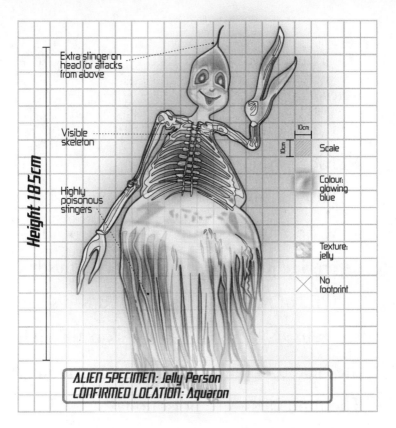

Extra stinger on head for attacks from above

Visible skeleton

Highly poisonous stingers

Height 185cm

10cm

10cm

Scale

Colour: glowing blue

Texture: jelly

No footprint

ALIEN SPECIMEN: Jelly Person
CONFIRMED LOCATION: Aquaron

'Great to meet you,' Kip said. It was best to be super-friendly when meeting new aliens.

Nurdor smiled with his mouth, but not with his glowing eyes.

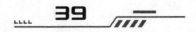

'The Jellies would like to throw you a *welcome party*.'

Kip thought he heard a funny edge to Nurdor's voice.

Finbar told Nurdor he shouldn't have gone to any fuss. But Nurdor wouldn't listen. He just flicked his tentacles busily.

One of the tentacles brushed Kip's leg. He yelped. Pain burned his skin through the SeaStocking, itching and throbbing. The tentacles were poisonous!

'So sorry,' Nurdor said briskly. 'This way, please.'

The Jelly turned and glided through the water. His jelly skirt rippled and his tentacles fanned out behind him like hair.

Rubbing his aching leg, Kip studied Nurdor from behind. He made Kip nervous. Still, the WorldCorp Manual of Space Scouting was clear.

SPACE SCOUT RULE 3.09(a):
Alien parties: a Space Scout must accept invitations from friendly aliens.

Kip and Finbar had a duty to follow Nurdor. And the party would be as good a way as any to check out Aquaron.

Nurdor set off through the city. Jellies were everywhere, all transparent and glowing blue.

'The glow's a kind of electrical charge,' Finbar whispered. 'Jellyfish on Earth produce it in their bodies. I think these Jellies are similar.'

They passed by a pole with a rotating dish. *Maybe the Jellies harness their electricity to power those dishes*, Kip thought. *Very sophisticated — especially since I don't think jellyfish have brains!*

Some Jellies glided by in pairs, tentacle-in-tentacle.

There were no vehicles on the Jellies' streets. They didn't need them, Kip figured. Not when they could glide around so quickly and easily.

When the passing Jellies saw Kip and

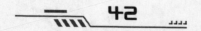

Finbar, they whispered to each other. Kip wondered what they were saying.

'We're here!' Nurdor snapped suddenly. 'The New Worker Centre.'

They were standing in front of a thick black door encrusted with pearl. When Nurdor floated up to it, it opened automatically.

'The New *Worker* Centre?' Kip echoed, confused.

'Er, the New *Party* Centre,' said Nurdor quickly.

They found themselves inside a pearl chamber. There were giant upturned clamshells on the floor. Beside them was a glittering golden chest.

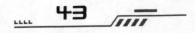

'Sit,' Nurdor said. It sounded like an order, not an invitation.

'Where are the other party guests?' Finbar asked suspiciously.

'Oh, they'll be here,' Nurdor said, his eyes darting around. 'But first, you need one of our traditional Aquaron body decorations. No party is complete without one.'

Kip and Finbar sank down onto the shells. Nurdor stood over them, his tentacles swishing.

Nurdor took a sharp, white needle made of shell from the chest. Then before Kip knew what was happening, Nurdor flicked his tentacles at Kip and Finbar's arms.

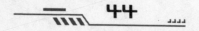

The pain was thousands of times stronger than when Nurdor had flicked Kip's leg. Kip couldn't move. His arms and legs were paralysed! Finbar could do nothing but howl.

Nurdor pushed the sleeve of Kip's SeaStocking up to his shoulder. Horrified, Kip watched as the Jelly poked the needle into his bare skin, over and over again.

Kip knew that if he could have felt the needle, it would have been torture.

Next, Nurdor grabbed Finbar's arm. Kip's head was spinning. His mission was out of control! He could only watch as Nurdor did exactly the same thing to Finbar through his fur.

'There's no party, is there?' Kip said, when he'd cleared his head. The movement in his arms was starting to return.

'Of course not,' Nurdor laughed. 'Fool.'

Kip inspected his shoulder. Underneath the skin, he could see the glowing blue shape of a Jelly. Nurdor had used the Jellies' own

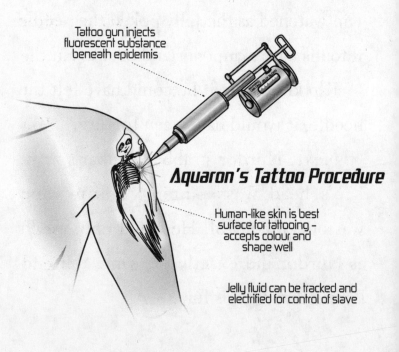

Tattoo gun injects fluorescent substance beneath epidermis

Aquaron's Tattoo Procedure

Human-like skin is best surface for tattooing – accepts colour and shape well

Jelly fluid can be tracked and electrified for control of slave

electrically charged fluid to make a tattoo!

'It's a tracking tattoo,' Nurdor said. 'Once you are above the surface, you're not allowed to go further than three kilometres from Jelly City.'

Those poles with rotating dishes, Kip guessed. *They're electrical trackers!*

'Go further and we'll send the eels after you. And if you spend too long above the water, the tattoo will *shock* you.'

We've got to get rid of these tattoos, Kip thought desperately. *Then get out of here!*

But Nurdor continued, as if reading Kip's mind. 'The tattoos can't be erased,' he said, cackling. 'You and your fluffy friend are slaves to the Jellies now!'

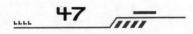

Nurdor took two black waterproof suits from the golden chest. He shook them out.

At once, the suits puffed up to the size of a chubby human body. Instead of zips there were watertight seals. The suits had helmets with clear panels to see through.

Chambers in suit inflate when filled with air or water

Super-expandable seaweed-like fabric

Aquaron AirSuit

Gloves and boots seal on to suit for watertightness

'These are AirSuits,' Nurdor said briskly. 'Climb in, swim to the surface and fill the suit with warm water.'

'Why?' Kip scowled.

'A SLAVE DOESN'T ASK QUESTIONS!'

Nurdor thundered.

But the Jelly seemed to want to prove to Kip how successful his alien race was. 'Sea Sprouts have made the Jellies fabulously rich,' Nurdor explained haughtily. 'We grow them all over our city.'

Those grey plants everywhere, with the square leaves, remembered Kip. *What's so special about them?*

'They're the most nutritious plant in any known galaxy,' Nurdor said. 'We trade them with other planets for millions.'

WorldCorp was right! Kip thought. *There is a valuable resource on Aquaron.*

That resource could probably feed humans…provided they didn't mind eating grey vegetables.

'The water down here is too cold to grow the Sea Sprouts?' Kip guessed. 'You need warm water from the surface.'

Nurdor muttered something. Kip's training had taught him to miss nothing. It sounded like Nurdor said, 'You're as smart as the King said you'd be.'

Why would the King have been talking about us? Kip wondered. *He had no way of knowing we were coming…did he?*

'Enough chat,' snapped Nurdor. He tossed the AirSuits to Kip and Finbar.

Kip's eyes narrowed. Putting on the AirSuit went against every instinct in Kip's body. He'd been trained for action,

to defend himself and help his people. Going along with Nurdor felt like giving up.

Still, Kip hadn't forgotten the pain of Nurdor's tentacle. One wrong step and Nurdor would sting him again. Or worse!

Kip pulled the AirSuit on over his SeaStocking. The AirSuit was heavy, and Kip's whole body felt clunky and useless.

'Hurry up,' Nurdor snapped at Finbar, whose furry paws were struggling with the seal on his suit.

Kip glared at Nurdor, and pulled the suit closed for Finbar.

Tentacles rippling, Nurdor led Kip and Finbar out of the pearl chamber. They made their way back through the city.

This time, Kip knew why the Jellies they passed were staring and whispering. As they went in and out of Jelly restaurants and bowling allies, the Jellies were sizing up their new slaves!

Kip's blood pumped hot in his veins.

All the Jellies do is have fun all day, he thought. *And it's because others are doing their work for them.*

They reached the entrance to the dome. Then Kip noticed something. The WaterWalker was gone! And Duke was still inside.

'Worried about your little friend?' Nurdor asked, seeing Kip stiffen.

'Where's Duke?' Kip asked, glaring at Nurdor.

'His Majesty might like Duke as a play-thing,' Nurdor said. 'Or perhaps for *dinner*.'

Kip's knees wobbled. His head throbbed. He thought being a slave to the Jellies was the absolute low point of his Space Scout career. But things had just gotten worse.

'Don't you *dare* hurt him,' Kip growled.

'Ah, little human,' Nurdor smiled. 'Soon

you will learn that the Jellies are superior. We do exactly what we want, when we want. Because we can.'

He pushed Kip and Finbar through the entrance and out into the open sea. 'Get to work,' Nurdor ordered. 'You have one hour to return with warm water. Your tattoo will pulse with electricity to remind you.'

The monster eels swam aside to let them pass. Kip and Finbar were on their own. But they were far from free.

CHAPTER 7

Since the Jellies could track them, there was no point plotting an escape yet. And there were too many Jellies for Kip and Finbar to take on alone.

Kip felt powerless, and he hated it. As far as he could see, their only option was to swim to the surface.

Teeth gritted, Kip launched himself

upwards. His AirSuit was uncomfortably hot with the SeaStocking on underneath. Plus he couldn't stop thinking about Duke. A million rescue plans popped into his head. None of them seemed possible, at least not with a Jelly tattoo on his arm.

Finbar followed Kip. Being a wolf, he hated water and wasn't used to swimming long distances. Back in Jelly City, Finbar had been using the only stroke he knew — doggy paddle. But it tired him out. He soon lagged behind Kip.

Kip paused, treading water until Finbar caught up. Then he noticed a long shape wriggling towards him. A giant leech!

Gross! Kip had completely forgotten

that the sea was infested with leeches.

Hurry up, Finbar! he thought desperately.

The leech wriggled towards Kip. Slowly, it wrapped itself around Kip's neck. It was looking for a way through his AirSuit to suck his blood!

Shuddering, Kip tried to pull it off. But the leech stuck fast. Working from the tail, Kip tried again. It took all of Kip's strength to rip the giant leech off his suit. But another was heading in his direction.

At last, Finbar paddled out from behind a transparent seaweed forest. Leeches crawled all over him.

Kip helped Finbar to rip them off. Then he grabbed Finbar under the arms and frog-kicked them both all the way to the surface. Luckily, fitness was one of Kip's strong points.

Finally, they burst through to the surface. They bobbed on the red water easily.

Above sea-level, Kip's SpaceCuff had reception again. He switched it on at once.

'Are you calling MoNa?' Finbar asked.

Kip thought for a moment. If MoNa sent two Scrambler Beams, he and Finbar could escape right then.

His mission was complete, because he knew what the Jellies were trading. And he was sure Aquaron wasn't Earth 2, not with the evil Jellies in control.

But if they escaped now, they'd have to

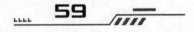

leave without Duke.

'I can't go. Not without my minisaur,' Kip said quietly.

He switched his SpaceCuff to Map Mode. An instant satellite image popped up on the screen.

'What's that?' Kip wondered out loud, studying the map.

Aquaron was covered by sea. But the SpaceCuff had picked up what seemed to be a group of tiny islands! Kip zoomed in. He saw the islands weren't rock, but woven reeds — and they were floating in the sea.

'Those islands are exactly three kilometres from Jelly City,' Finbar said, looking over Kip's shoulder.

'Maybe there are other slaves there!' Kip said. 'They can't go any further than that.'

Kip wasn't sure the other slaves would be friendly. And they had less than an hour above the water to find out.

But hope soared inside Kip anyway. Other slaves would know more about the Jellies. They might be able to help rescue Duke!

Bobbing in their AirSuits, Kip and Finbar swam towards the islands. They soon came into view. Kip was right! There were figures on top, all wearing AirSuits. More slaves. Finbar's superior wolf vision saw every detail.

The aliens were shaped like humans, but each had four eyes instead of two.

Swimming a final stroke, Kip grabbed onto the reed island. One of the aliens reached down to help Kip up.

'Hello, I'm Virgil,' said the alien. 'I am a Gird.' Just like the Jellies, Virgil spoke Kip's language perfectly.

'These are some of my people,' Virgil said, waving a hand around the small island. Kip counted twenty more Girds.

'The others are collecting water for the Jellies,' Virgil said. 'Like you, we're slaves.'

Kip introduced himself. He explained to Virgil what he and Finbar were doing on Aquaron.

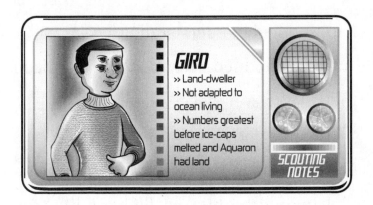

GIRD
» Land-dweller
» Not adapted to ocean living
» Numbers greatest before ice-caps melted and Aquaron had land

SCOUTING NOTES

Then Virgil told Kip the story of Aquaron. 'Once, Girds and Jellies shared this planet peacefully,' said Virgil. 'Aquaron was icy. Girds lived on the land and Jellies in the sea.'

Virgil explained how a meteorite had knocked Aquaron out of orbit, pushing it closer to the sun. The ice had melted, covering Aquaron in an ocean.

'Then the Jellies took over?' guessed

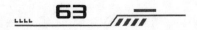

Kip, suddenly understanding.

Virgil nodded. 'My people have been their slaves ever since,' he said.

Kip imagined life as a Gird. No freedom. Nothing but endless work and misery.

It would be his and Finbar's life too, if Kip didn't do something to stop it.

CHAPTER 8

Questions flooded Kip's brain. The Jellies didn't *need* slaves. They were obviously smart enough to work out how to pump warm water from the surface.

Virgil put a hand on Kip's shoulder. He seemed to know what Kip was struggling to understand. 'They keep us as slaves to show us that they're more powerful.'

Kip was about to reply when his SpaceCuff buzzed.

MESSAGE FROM MoNa 4000

BREAKTHROUGH
WorldCorp's techs have traced the mysterious coded messages. They came from below the sea on Aquaron itself!

Incoming message

MoNa's message didn't make sense! She seemed to be saying the Jellies sent the messages to WorldCorp. But why would they want Earthlings to know about their trade in Sea Sprouts?

Unless…

Kip shivered. *The Jellies sent those messages to lure us here*, he thought. *Humans are known throughout the galaxies for being smart. By making us slaves, the Jellies could prove that they're smarter.*

Once Kip looked for it, the evidence was clear. The whirlpool, for example – it could have been made by the Jellies' giant propellers. It was designed to suck Kip and Finbar under the water.

Now Kip was sure of one thing. *The Jellies were expecting us!*

Kip seethed. Being a slave was terrible. Walking into a trap was worse.

Kip's tracking tattoo began to tingle with electricity. Time was running out! If they didn't get back down to Jelly City with a suit full of warm water soon, the

eels would come after them.

But there had to be *something* he could do to take back control.

'We've got to erase the tattoos,' Kip said firmly.

'Girds have been trying for years,' replied Virgil, shaking his head. 'It is painful to have part of the Jellies inside us.'

'The fluid is like the Jellies' version of blood,' Finbar said, thinking aloud.

Kip said nothing for a second, but his mind was racing. Then –

'That's it, Finbar!' Kip suddenly yelled.

'The fluid is like blood!'

Finbar, Virgil and the rest of the Girds looked at Kip like he was mad.

'The giant leeches under the surface!' Kip added. 'Maybe they can suck the Jelly fluid out of our arms.'

Virgil shook his head. 'Your plan won't work,' he said. 'The Death Slugs are poisonous. If they touch your skin, you'll die instantly.'

'Death Slugs?' Kip said, puzzled. 'They just look like leeches.'

Kip thought back to Space Scout training. He remembered a long, boring lecture called Identifying Alien Sea Creatures. He never thought the lecture would be

important. But now, it was coming in very handy…

Without another word, Kip leapt off the floating reed island. He took off his gloves and disappeared under the water.

Holding his breath, Kip dived down. He spotted a leech wriggling past. He scooped up the leech and shot back up to the surface.

Kip burst out of the water. The leech had attached itself to Kip's hand and started sucking his blood. Kip held out his hand to the others.

'See? Gross, but harmless.'

'But…the Jellies told us they were deadly,' Virgil stammered.

Of course they did, Kip thought grimly.

He plucked the leech from his hand. Rolling up the sleeves of his AirSuit and Sea Stocking, Kip put the leech on his tattoo.

The Girds watched in silence as the leech sucked Kip's skin. The leech swelled up to three, then four times its size. But instead of sucking Kip's blood, the leech was sucking out the Jelly fluid. In seconds, Kip's tattoo was gone.

'Let me try,' said Virgil.

The other Girds watched as Virgil picked the bloated leech off Kip's arm and put it on his own tattoo.

'It's working!' Virgil said, as his tattoo disappeared.

Finbar and the rest of the Girds jumped into the water to grab their own leeches. Soon, everyone was erasing the hated Jelly tattoos.

They were all free!

Well, everyone except Duke.

CHAPTER 9

'Now that we're free, we need to go back down to Jelly City,' Kip said to Finbar.

Finbar was a loyal 2iC, and he nodded.

They both knew it would be extremely dangerous. But Kip already had a plan in mind.

Jumping back into the water, he opened the valve on his AirSuit. Warm water

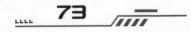

gushed in. The suit swelled to twice its size and weight. Finbar filled his suit too.

Kip's plan was to pretend they had fetched water like good Jelly slaves. That would be the easiest way back into the city.

It was time to say goodbye to Virgil and the other Girds.

'What will you do now?' Kip asked Virgil.

'Thanks to you, we're free to move around our planet again,' said Virgil. 'We'll build our floating city far away from the Jellies. The Girds will become strong again.'

Waving goodbye, Kip and Finbar dived

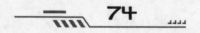

into the red sea. In their heavy AirSuits, the trip down to the sea floor was easy. With their arms and legs in the pin-drop position, they sank like stones.

Jelly City soon loomed up below them. Kip and Finbar swam through the entrance, past the eels with their glittering dagger teeth.

Nurdor was waiting for them. He didn't look happy.

Beside Nurdor was a giant barrel with a hose attached. Nurdor fitted the hose to Kip's AirSuit. He drained the warm water from Kip's suit, then Finbar's.

Luckily, Nurdor couldn't see they had erased their tattoos because their arms

were covered by their suits.

'Too slow, slaves,' Nurdor said. 'You've made me angry.' He flicked one of his poisoned tentacles towards them.

'We'll do better next time,' Kip said, fingers crossed behind his back.

'Next time will have to wait,' Nurdor snapped. 'Your pesky minisaur has escaped. He won't obey anyone! The King wants minisaur chops for dinner. You must catch your bratty pet for him.'

Kip shot a glance at Finbar. This was their chance to save Duke!

'Go to the King's Palace immediately,' Nurdor said. 'And don't even think of escaping. Remember, we can track you.'

That's what you think, Kip answered silently.

Kip and Finbar set off, half-swimming, half-walking again through Jelly City. The King's Palace was easy to spot. It was the biggest, shiniest tower in the whole city. A giant black pearl carved into the shape of a crown sat at the top of the tower.

Ignoring the stares of passing Jellies, Kip and Finbar swam quickly through the city. Outside the palace, Kip found a cage made of strange bones. Duke had chewed through it like a pair of spaceboots. He was nowhere to be seen.

'How's he breathing under water?' Kip asked Finbar. Then it struck him. 'Oh, of

course! Duke's amphibious.'

Some reptiles were, like crocodiles.

Kip still had Duke's sonic leash in the pocket of his normal clothes. Frantically, he reached under the layers of his AirSuit and SeaStocking to dig it out. Luckily, the sonic leash was waterproof.

Kip seriously doubted the leash would work. Duke never obeyed it in Dino-Training classes! But Kip switched it to the Call Dino setting anyway.

The sonic leash sent out its ultra high-frequency sound, which only Duke could hear.

Kip and Finbar waited. Nothing. Duke was nowhere to be seen.

Then…

OOMPH!

Out of nowhere, a solid green shape leapt into Kip's arms. Duke!

'Stop it, boy!' Kip laughed, as Duke tried to lick Kip's face through his AirSuit. He was relieved to see Duke again, but he put his pet down. 'We've got to leave right now!'

Ignoring him, Duke rolled over and played dead. This was worse than Dino-Training! They really had to get out of there.

'Come with us now,' said Finbar slowly, 'and you'll never have to go back to Dino-Training.'

At once, Duke jumped up and raced over to Kip's side.

Who said minisaurs aren't smart? Kip and Finbar smiled at each other.

Kip quickly hid Duke inside his AirSuit.

Now all they had to do was escape Jelly City!

CHAPTER 10

Kip and Finbar half-ran, half-swam back through the city. Nurdor was waiting for them at the entrance.

'Did you find the minisaur?' he growled.

Duke's tail tickled Kip's neck.

'Um…no,' Kip said.

'That's just great,' said Nurdor sarcastically. 'Now I'll have to find the King something else for dinner. He'll be furious.'

He stared at Kip with glowing blue eyes. 'Wait! What's that bulge in your AirSuit?' Nurdor asked, tentacles on his hips.

'Oh, it's nothing,' said Kip.

'It's shaped exactly like a minisaur!' Nurdor hissed.

'SWIM FOR IT!' Kip yelled.

Kip and Finbar surged past Nurdor and out of the city. The other Jellies stared.

'After them!' Nurdor screeched at the Jellies nearby.

Kip was already exhausted. They'd been

swimming for hours. But he gathered every shred of energy he had left. This time, they were swimming for their lives.

'Remember, Earthlings,' Nurdor yelled at Kip and Finbar. 'There is no escape!'

Just watch us, Nurdor, Kip thought.

Kip and Finbar swam for the surface. Kip's lungs burned. He couldn't seem to get enough air in through his mask.

But that didn't matter. They had to go on. The Jellies were still behind them!

At last, Kip and Finbar broke through to the surface of the water. Kip dialled MoNa on his SpaceCuff.

Nurdor will go crazy when he realises we've escaped, Kip thought. He smiled, imagining Nurdor's furious expression.

'Send two Scramblers ASAP!' he said urgently, when MoNa answered.

'And a Scrambler for your WaterWalker, too?' MoNa asked.

The WaterWalker! Kip had totally

forgotten about it. There was no way he was heading back to Jelly City to get it.

'Er… we had a little technical problem with the WaterWalker,' Kip said. 'I'll explain when we're on board.'

Seconds ticked by. Then suddenly, two Scrambler Beams shot down from above.

Relieved, Kip and Finbar splashed into the beams, just as Kip caught sight of the Jellies gliding angrily through the water towards them. Kip had time to wave goodbye before the Scramblers hit.

Instantly, Kip had the feeling that something was taking his body apart, cell by cell, and shuffling bits all over the place. No matter how many times he travelled by

Scrambler, he never got used to it.

So long, Aquaron! he thought, dazed.

The next thing he knew, Kip was lying in a puddle in MoNa's landing bay.

Finbar was next to him, his wet fur clinging to him. They pulled off their AirSuits, the last sign they'd ever been slaves to the Jellies. Kip was glad to get back into his comfy dry spacesuit.

Immediately, Kip and Finbar headed for the bridge. Kip had to file his mission report.

When they got there, Kip settled into his captain's chair. His holographic consol appeared around him. Kip began typing on the mid-air keyboard.

CAPTAIN'S LOG
Aquaron

Climate: Once icy but now covered in water.

Population: Very rich, very evil aliens called Jellies. They are giant, mean Jellyfish. Also Girds, a gentle race of four-eyed humanoids. Until recently, the Jellies had enslaved the Girds.

Recommendation: The Jellies are trading nutritious vegetables called Sea Sprouts. This has made the Jellies rich. The Jellies would definitely not be willing to share their vegetables with humans, let alone their whole planet. Aquaron is definitely not Earth 2.

> **Note:** I must also report that the Jellies stole my WaterWalker. This proves yet again that they are not to be trusted.

KIP KIRBY, SPACE SCOUT #50

CLASSIFIED

CLASSIFIED

'Phew,' Kip sighed, hitting Send.

Work was over, for this mission at least. Kip was dying to check the Space Scout intranet. There'd be lots of gossip from other missions to catch up on. Plus, rankings on the Planetary Points Leader Board would have been updated.

With his report filed and the mission complete, Kip had earned one Planetary Point. He hadn't found Earth 2 yet. He just hoped no other Space Scout had either. Otherwise, his chance at the Shield of Honour would be gone.

'You're not a slave to your job, Kip,' Finbar said to him, as though he knew what Kip was thinking. 'Maybe it's time to relax?'

Kip grinned. 'Let's take Duke to the Virtu-Park,' he said.

Duke's ears pricked up.

Kip, Finbar and Duke headed for MoNa's Virtu-Park, which was near the bridge.

The Virtu-Park was a bit like the Air-Parks on Earth, except that it was in a sealed chamber on MoNa. Inside, the air was climate-controlled so the temperature was always a perfect 27 degrees.

A UV-free artificial sun shone down from the ceiling. Grass made of shredded silk carpeted the floor. There was even a soundtrack of birds tweeting piped through hidden surround-sound speakers.

Kip dug around in his spacesuit pocket.
He found a slightly mangled DinoTreat.

Suitable for
minisaurs and
meerkats

Remote paging
system for easy
retrieval of lost stick

Every box of DinoTreats comes
with a free AstroStick!

Drool-repellant
coating

'Jump, boy!' called Kip. He threw the
DinoTreat into the air. It spun in mid-air,
never dropping to the ground. The Virtu-

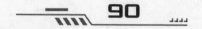

Park had a zero-gravity atmosphere. Duke rushed over. But he didn't jump up and grab the DinoTreat. Instead, he jumped into Finbar's arms and licked his face.

'Don't you ever do what you're told?' Finbar laughed.

Kip couldn't help smiling. Duke was definitely the naughtiest minisaur in space.

But that was fine by Kip. It was better that Duke was free to do things his own way. It was exactly how Kip liked things, too.

THE END